Alfred H. Howard

The Chest-Weight Manual

Alfred H. Howard

The Chest-Weight Manual

ISBN/EAN: 9783337340094

Printed in Europe, USA, Canada, Australia, Japan

Cover: Foto ©Andreas Hilbeck / pixelio.de

More available books at **www.hansebooks.com**

—THE—

◇CHEST-WEIGHT◇

MANUAL

PANION TO THE BOSTON G

BOSTON

several years. I am persuaded that no teacher of gymnastics has probed so nearly to the secret of physical remedy and improvement; certainly no one has more determinately engaged himself to discover the true and discard the false system of physical culture.

If I have succeeded in incorporating in this Manual some of the principles which I have learned from Mr. Roberts, that will be its highest merit and recommendation.

A. H. HOWARD.

BOSTON, 1887.

SUGGESTIONS.

1. At first, exercise only for short time, and use light weights.

Later, it would be well to practice twenty or thirty minutes each day. Even an hour a day, divided into two sessions of thirty minutes each, can be employed to advantage.

2. Familiarize the exercise as soon as possible, so as to avoid the necessity of referring to the Manual.

3. The benefit to be derived from the chest-weight exercise may be doubled by a quick sponge bath in tepid water, after finishing. A robust or full-blooded person may finish his bath in colder water.

4. There is no danger in taking a sponge bath while in a perspiration, provided it be done quickly. A tub bath is not so free from danger.

5. In the notes accompanying the following diagrams, it is repeatedly urged upon the pupil to "count," and to keep "arms straight and stiff." It is thought by this reiteration to force the observance of these cardinal rules of chest-weight practice.

6. Whenever "Position" is mentioned in the following notes, the particular position of the arms in the first cut of the book is what is referred to.

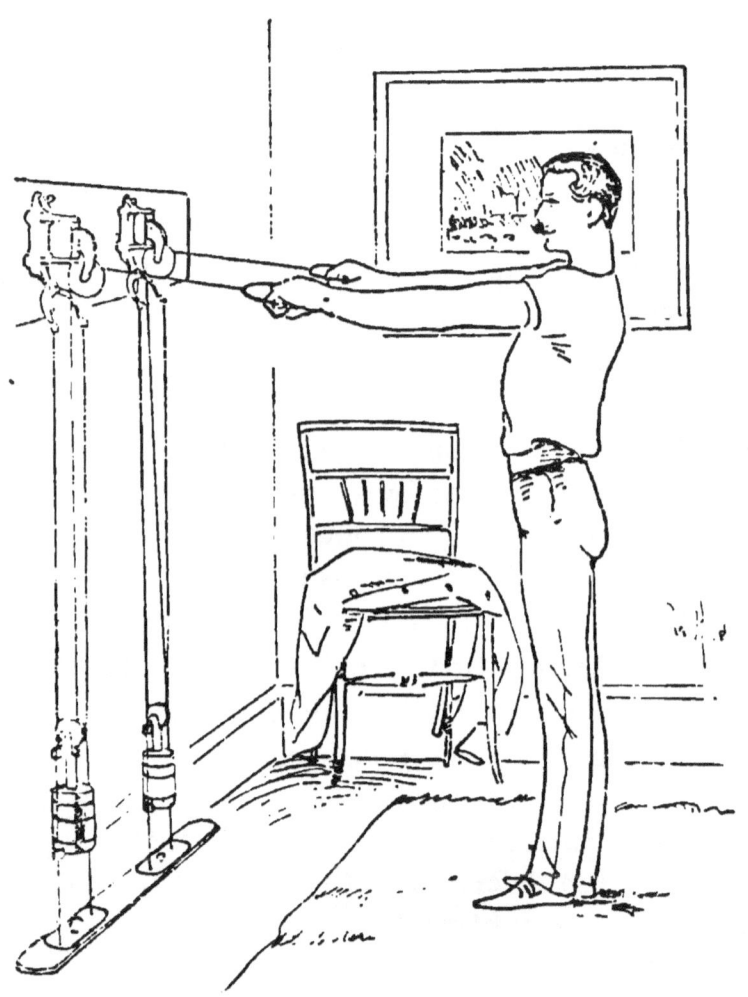

POSITION.

Preparatory to taking the exercise suggested in the following pages, the student should, after adjusting the weights to suit his strength, take position as in cut above, observing that

1. Body and head are erect, and chest thrown forward.

2. Heels are about nine inches apart.

3. Weights are lifted about twelve inches from the floor.

4. Feet are *never* placed one in front of the other.

5. Arms and cords are on a straight line from the shoulder to the swivel-wheel. Knuckles up.

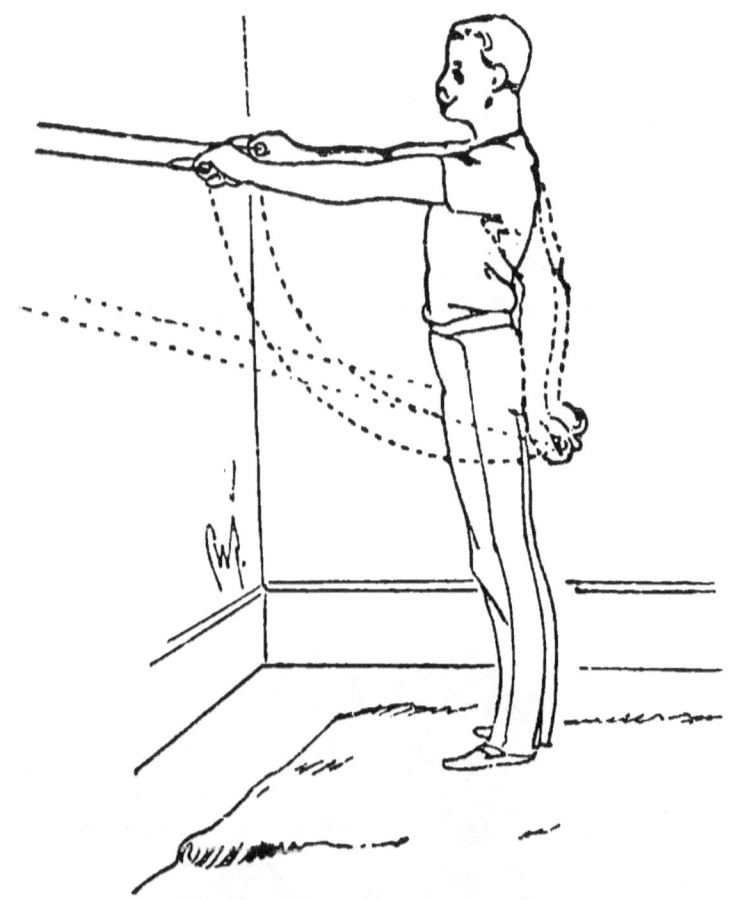

FIRST SERIES.
(*Facing the Machine.*)

1. Carry hands simultaneously down to the side, and a little past the line of the body. Count one as hands arrive at end of the movement, and two as they return to Position. Continue through sixteen counts. One half of the benefit of this exercise, and the other straight-arm movements to follow, will be lost if the arms are not kept *rigidly straight.*

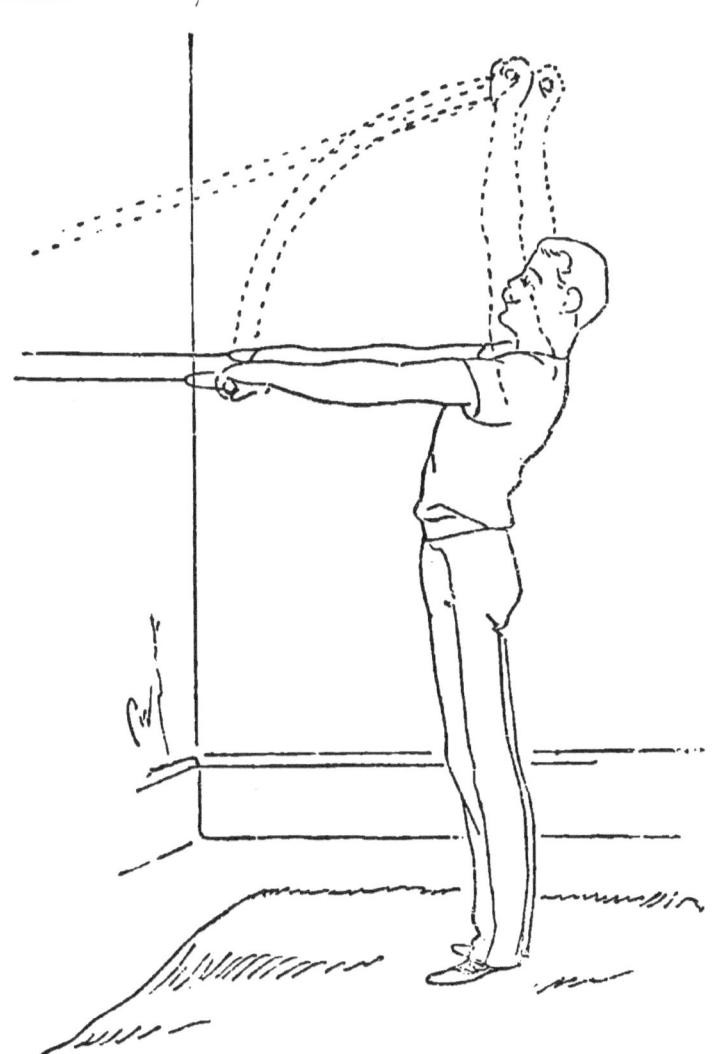

2. Carry arms up to perpendicular. Count one as they go up, and two as they return to Position, etc. Sixteen counts. Arms should pass up close to the head, biceps touching the ears. This movement can be recommended for stoop-shoulders.

All the exercises can be rendered doubly effective if the operator will continually pinch the handle as if to crush it.

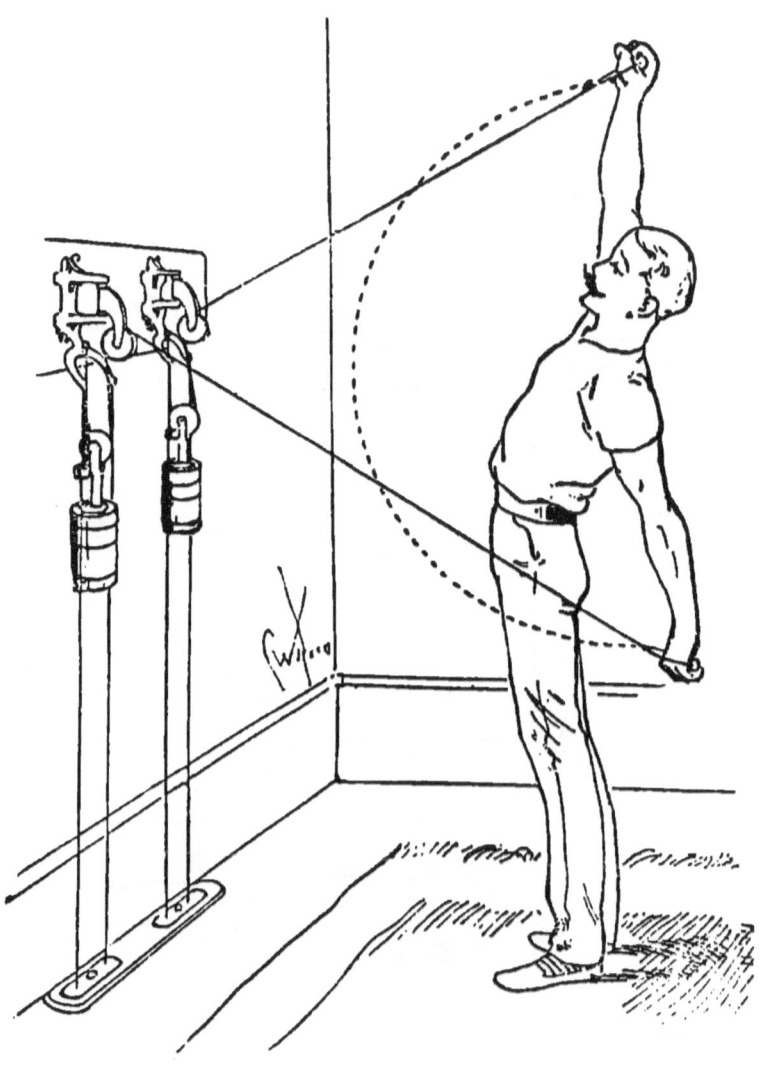

3. Hands start from Position, front horizontal, and move simultaneously in opposite directions, right going up and left down.   Count one as they reach opposite ends of semi-circle, two as they, returning, meet and pass at Position, and three as left reaches upper end, and right lower end of curve, etc.   Sixteen counts.

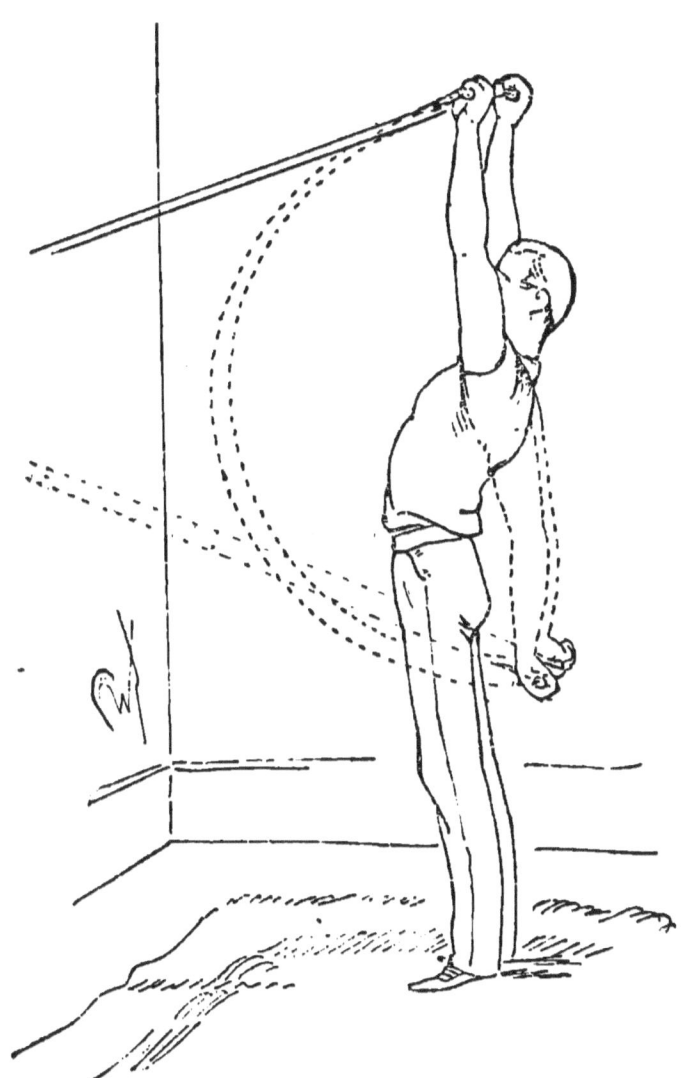

4. Combination of Nos. 1 and 2. Count one as hands go down, and two as they return, and pause at Position; three as they go up, etc. Sixteen counts. Always accent odd numbers in counting.

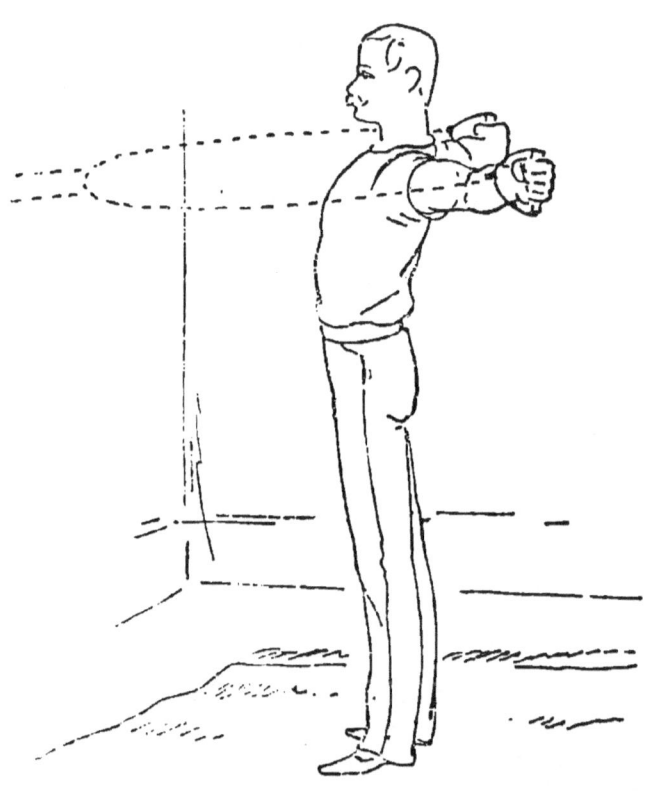

5. From Position carry each arm horizontally to its own side, knuckles out, arms rigidly straight, and always the height of the shoulders. Count and accent as heretofore. This exercise is especially helpful to round shoulders.

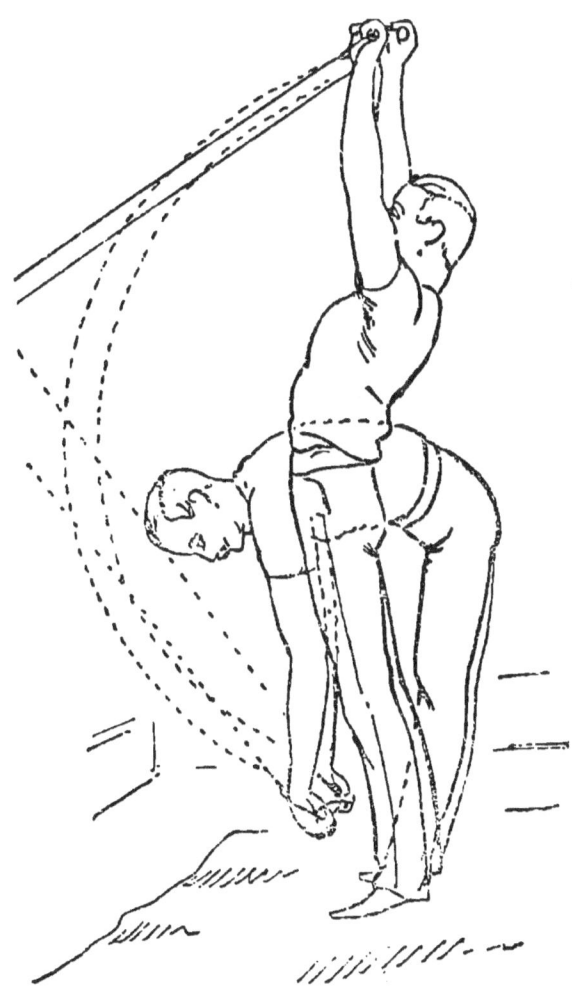

6. From Position carry hands down to toes, count one; back to Position, count two; high over head, count three, etc. Sixteen counts.

In downward motion, body should bend at hips *only*; knees stiff; arms throughout this exercise also should not bend.

7. From Position carry arms horizontally around to left side, count one; return to Position, count two; carry to right side, count three, etc. Sixteen counts. Arms should be straight, parallel, and horizontal.

The feet *should not* turn on the floor in the side movement; upper part of the body *should* turn (not arms simply). Strong waist action.

8. Spread feet far apart. From Position carry stiff arms down and between the legs, going as far back as possible, count one; return to Position, count two; carry stiff arms and upper body in semi-circle, as far back as possible, keeping legs straight, count three; return to Position, count four, etc. Sixteen counts.

Supplementary Combinations.

(a) Swing down between legs, as in No. 8, count one; and in coming up swing directly to left horizontal, as in No. 7; count two. Then swing down between

legs again, count three; and in coming up swing directly to left horizontal, count four, etc. Sixteen counts.

(b)   Likewise lower movement of No. 8 can be combined with No. 5.   In this and in *(a)* count two should be made, as arms reach side horizontal, and Position should not (as heretofore) be marked by a count.

(c)   No. 7 and No. 5 can each be thrown in between the two parts of No. 4.

The operator will be able to discover other combinations.

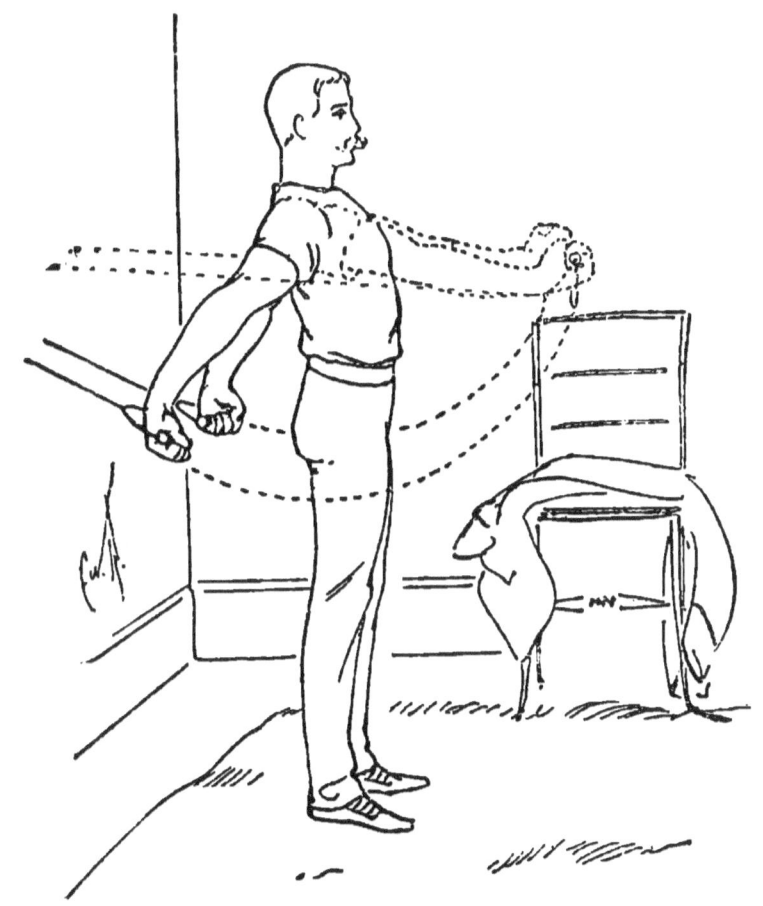

SECOND SERIES.

(Face from Machine.)

10. Carry hands forward, palms leading, arms straight. Count sixteen, as heretofore.

As arms go up on last count they should gradually turn, and arrive at front horizontal with knuckles up, ready for movement on next page.

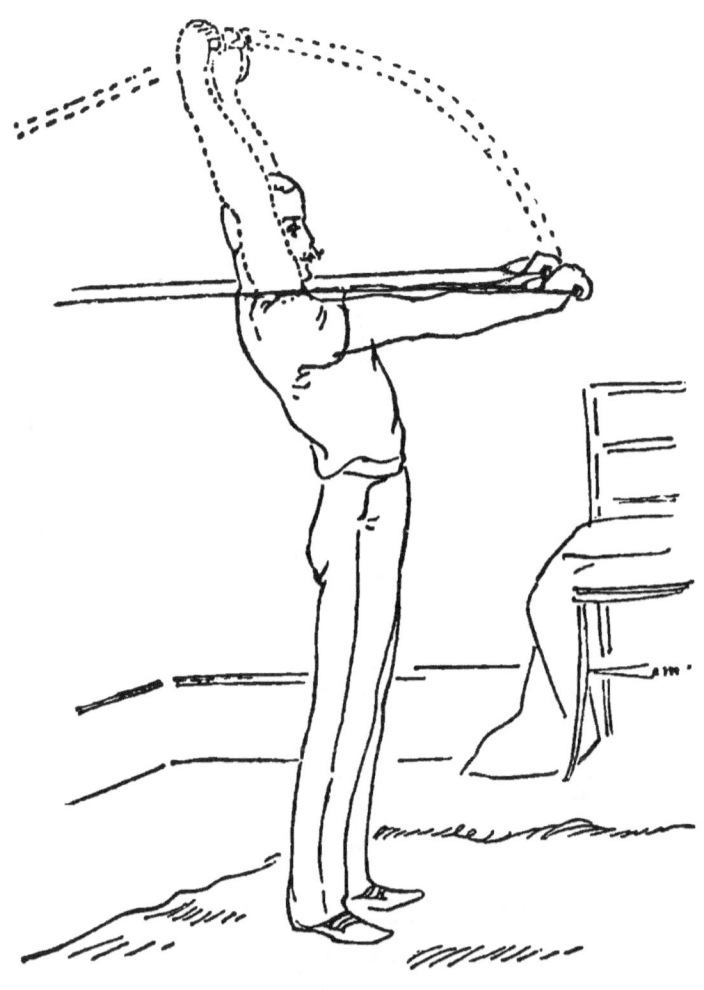

11. Body should be inclined well forward, so that it will not be pulled out of balance by the weights as the hands go up.   Sixteen counts.

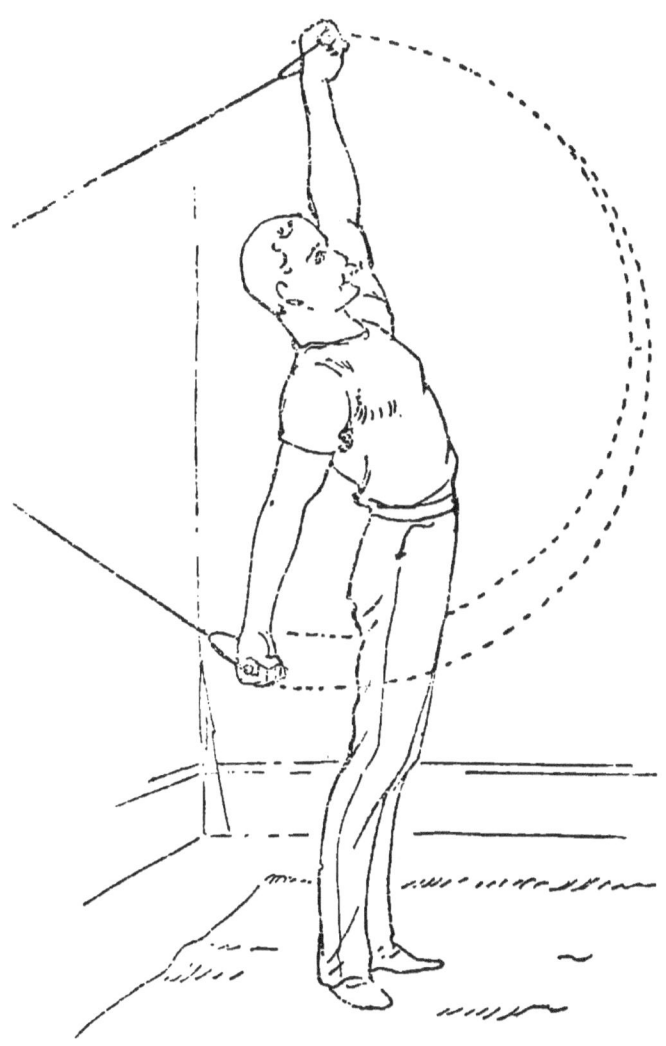

12. Arms start from front horizontal, and move in opposite directions, right going down and left up; count one as they arrive at extremes of semi-circle; count two as they, returning, meet and pass each other at front horizontal; count three as right arrives overhead and left below.

13. This exercise is a combination of 10 and 11. As the hands go down, let them gradually turn the knuckles downward. Count one as hands reach lower extremity of semicircle, etc. Sixteen counts.

14. Strictly a forearm movement. The upper arm takes horizontal position, and *holds* it, the elbow not being allowed to sink. By this means the triceps and muscles of the forearm are brought into vigorous action.

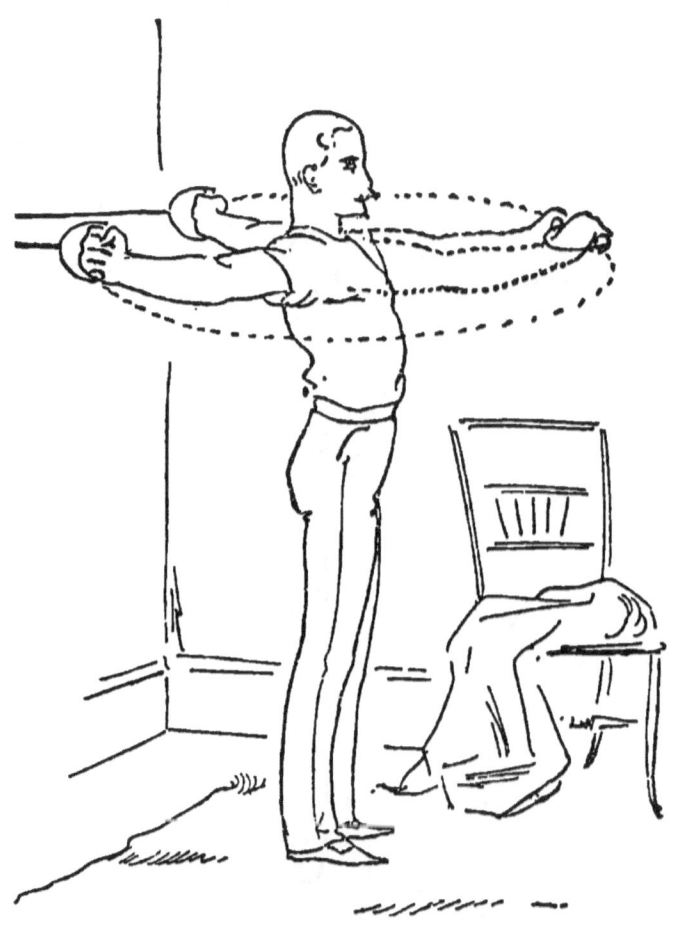

15.　Arms should not be allowed to sag, but be kept on horizontal plane, level with the shoulders.

Count one as hands go back, and two as they reach front, horizontal, etc.　Sixteen counts.

(*a*)　A new combination can be made by combining No. 10, No. 15, and No. 11.

(*b*)　The pupil will discover other combinations.

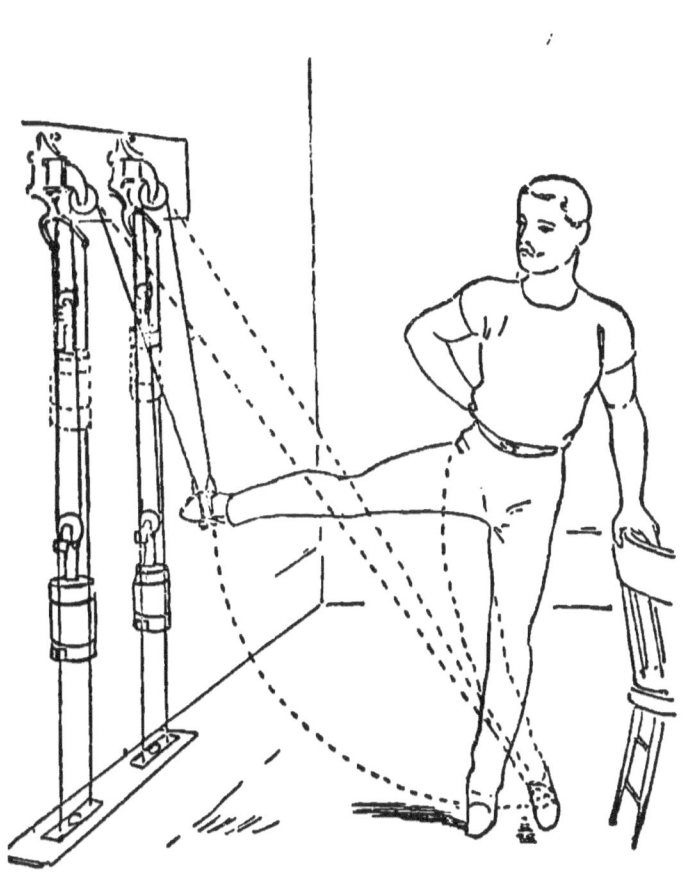

16. As leg moves slowly downward, count one, and two as it returns to horizontal.

In this movement the muscles of the inside thigh are exercised. Take same with other leg.

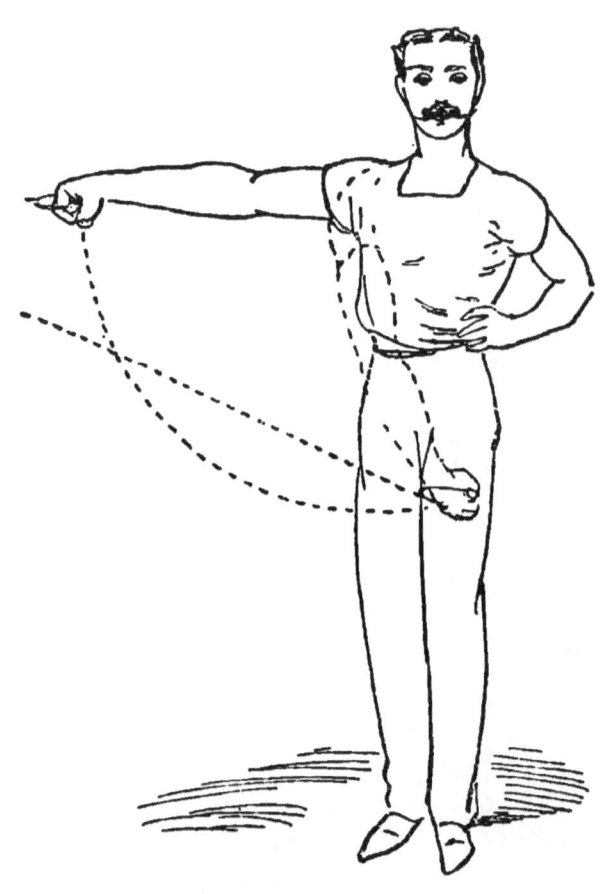

THIRD SERIES.

(Single Arm.)

17. Standing with right side toward machine, carry right hand down to left thigh, count one; as arm returns to horizontal, count two, etc. Sixteen counts. Don't forget to crush the handle!

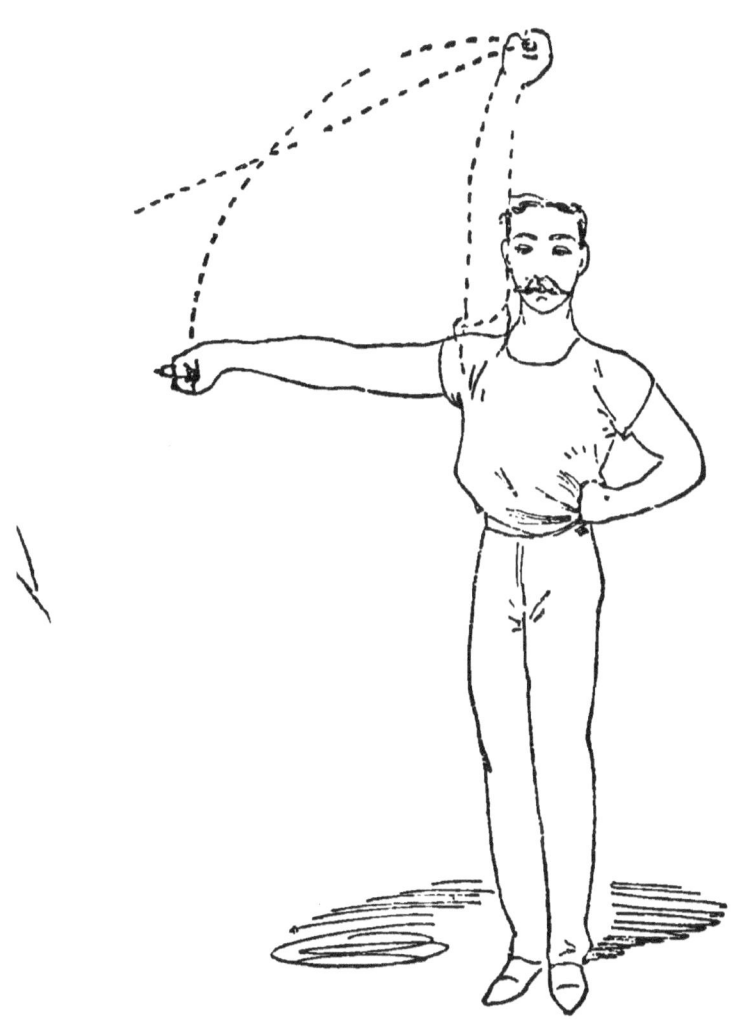

18. Biceps should touch ear as arm goes up, and body should not sway to the left. Count as usual.

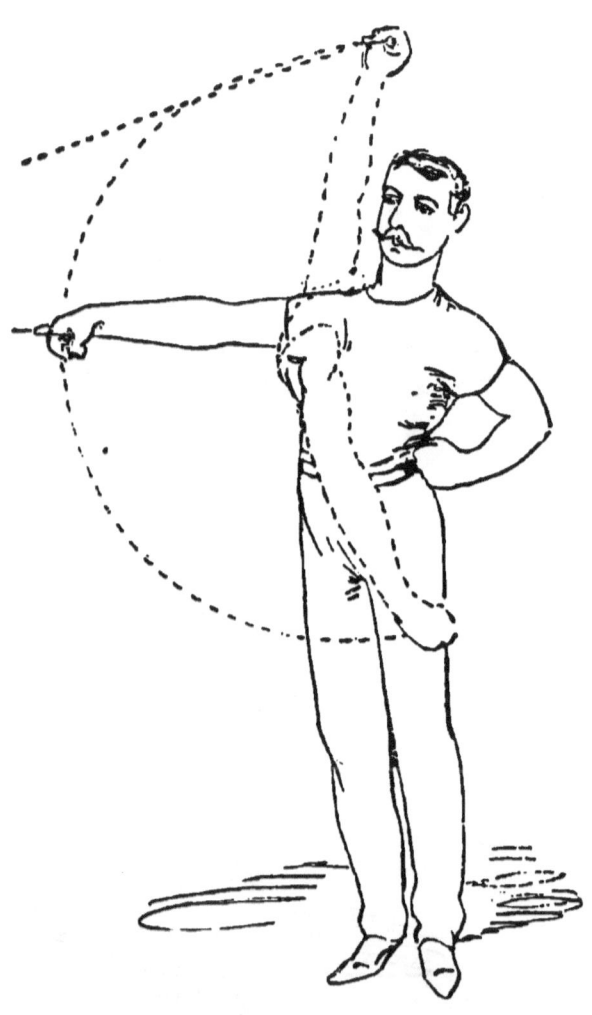

19. This exercise combines the two previous movements. Count one as hand goes down, two as it returns to horizontal, three as it goes up, etc. Sixteen counts.

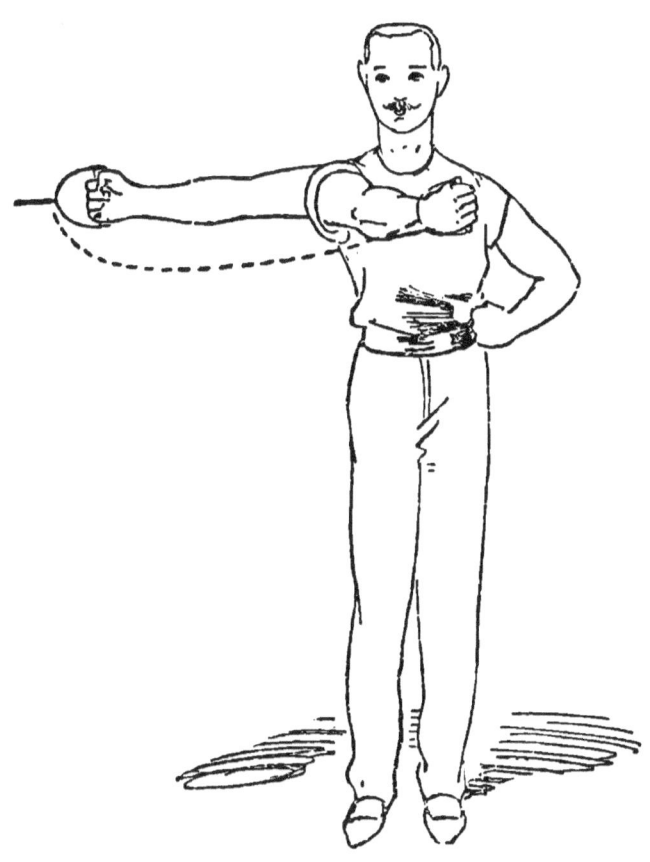

20. In this exercise body should remain motionless; the arm *alone* moves. Count as usual.

While still holding handle at side, horizontal, make a "right-about face," and let the arm take position as on next page, with left side toward machine.

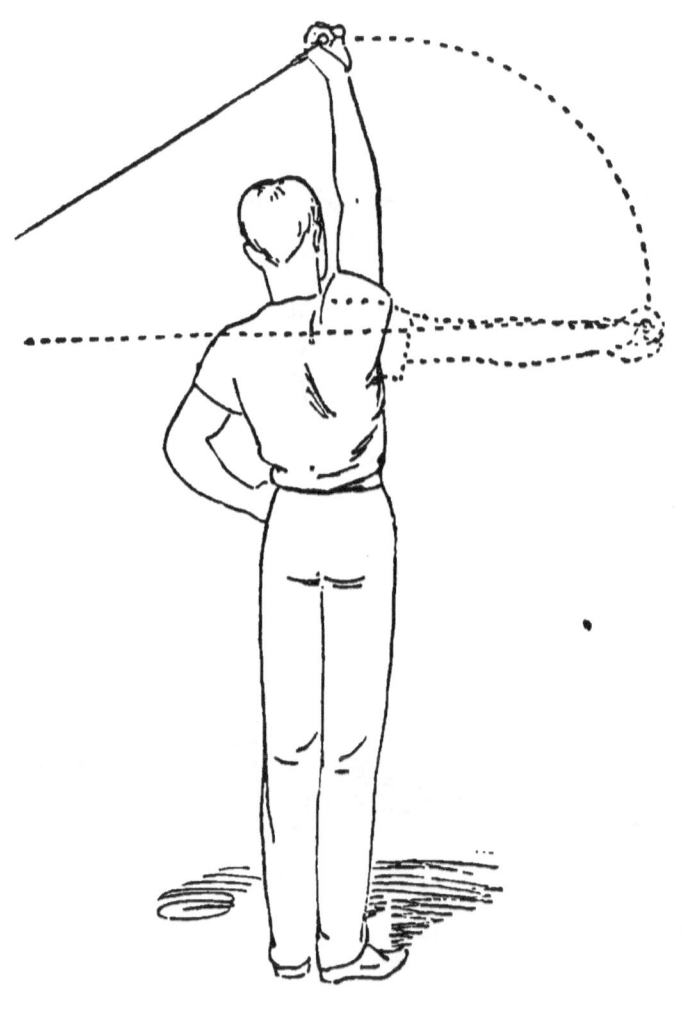

21. Body should remain erect and motionless; let arm do the work. As hand goes down, let cord pass back of head. Count as usual.

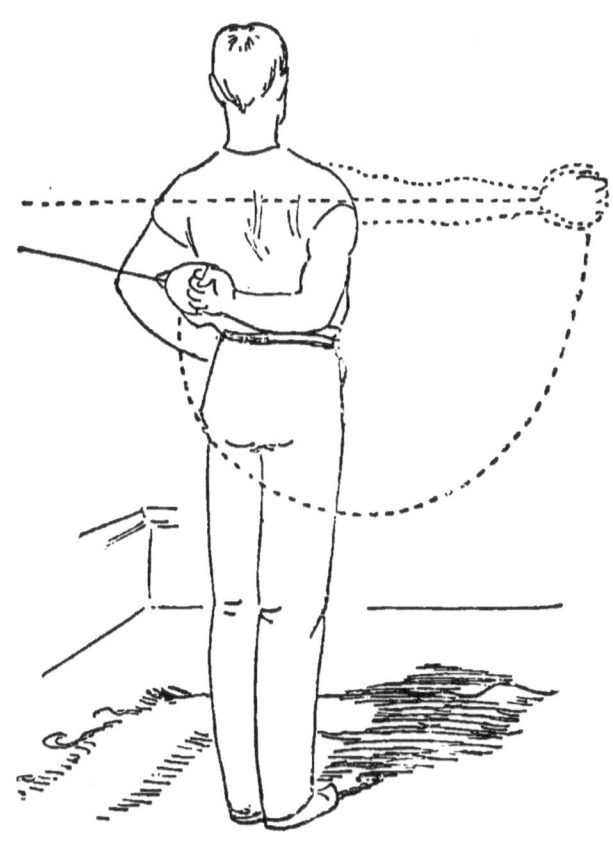

22. When the arm, passing down, begins to bend at the elbow, the wrist should twist, so that at the end of the stroke the palm will be turned out as in cut above. Sixteen counts, as usual.

This movement exercises wrist and deltoid.

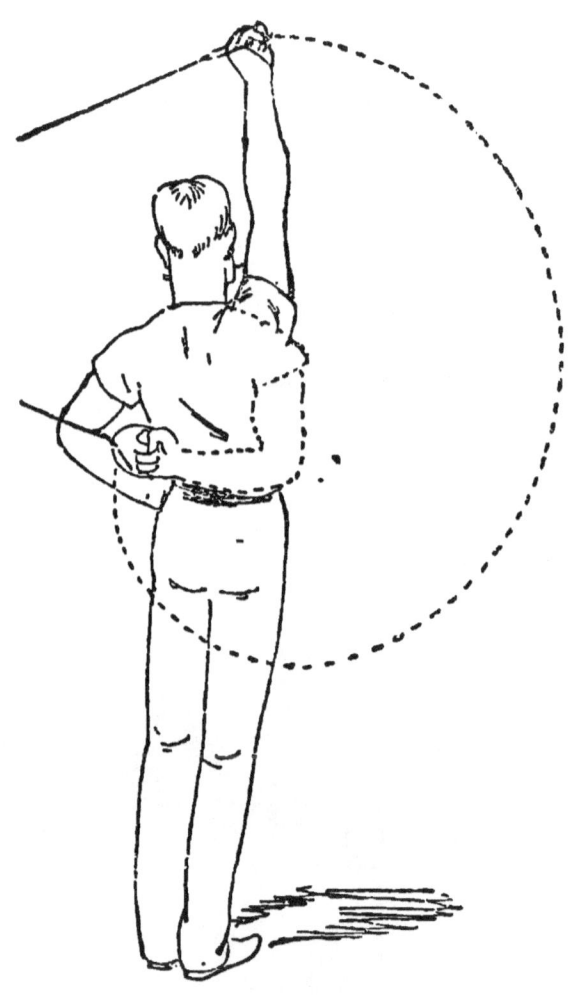

23. This movement combines two previous exercises. The wrist should gradually twist throughout the entire movement.

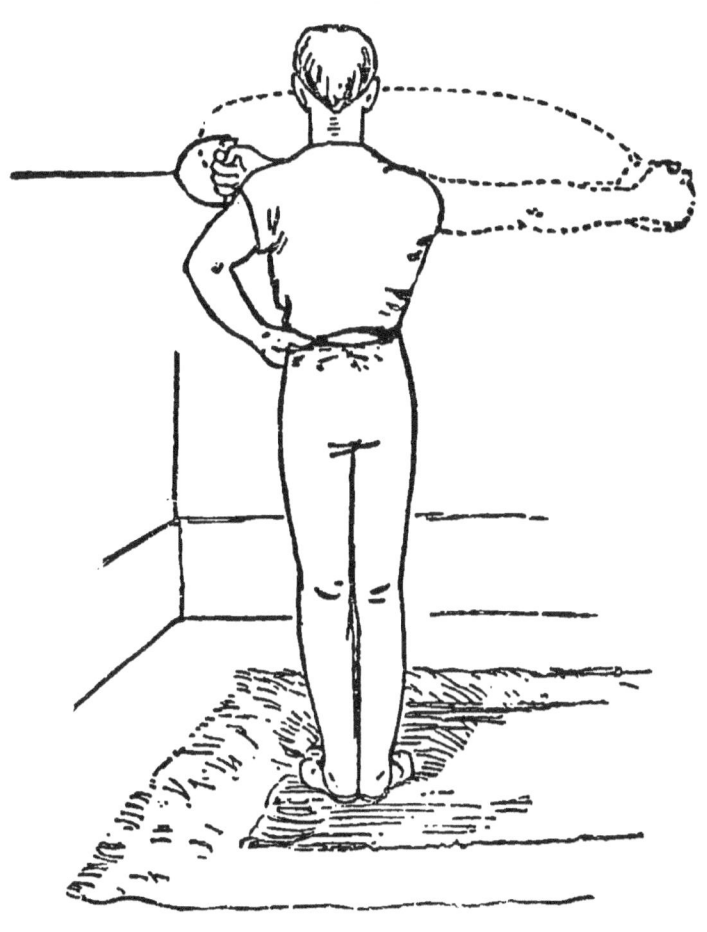

24. Let the right arm, which is stretched across the chest, move forward and to the right, keeping arm as straight as possible. Sixteen counts, as usual.

While body is in this position let left hand take the handle, and begin with single-arm exercise, No. 17. Execute the whole series with left hand.

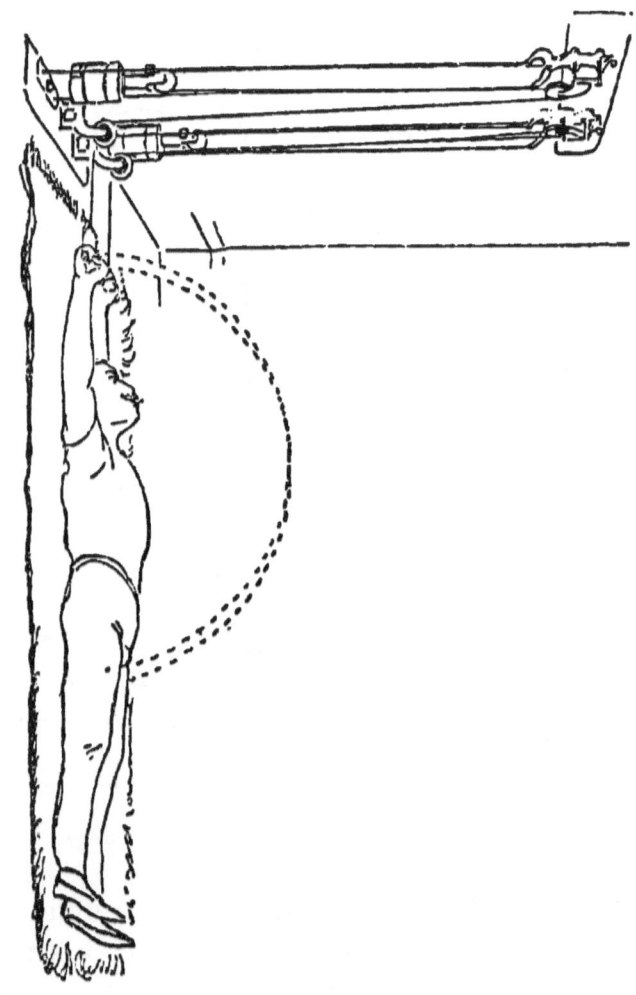

FOURTH SERIES.

(*Abdominal Attachment.*)

25. If the machine which the operator uses has a
rowing attachment, it will be noticed that the lower
swivel can be raised and lowered. When he is about
to take the abdominal exercises, the lower swivel should

be dropped as near the floor as possible. For the rowing exercises it should be raised as high as possible.

Lie on a mat (as in cut on preceding page) on the floor at such distance from the machine, that when the hands grasp the handles the weights will be a little raised from the floor. Let the arms, stiff and straight, start upward and forward, as per dotted lines in cut opposite. Execute this movement slowly. Count as in preceding series.

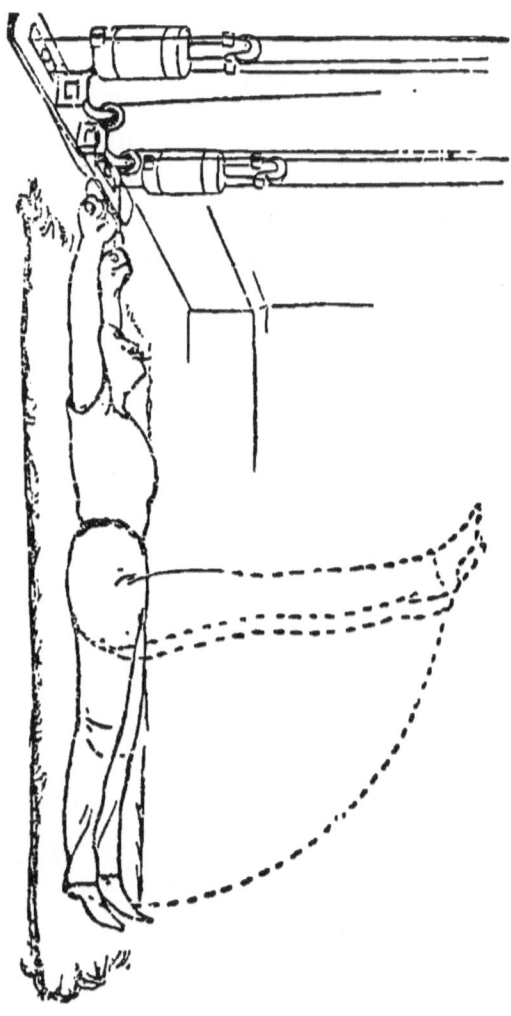

26. The legs should be rigidly stiff and straight, and should move upward from floor *very slowly*. It is impossible to make them move too slowly.

Three or four counts at first. This is one of the most effectual exercises in developing the abdominal muscles—a sure cure for dyspepsia.

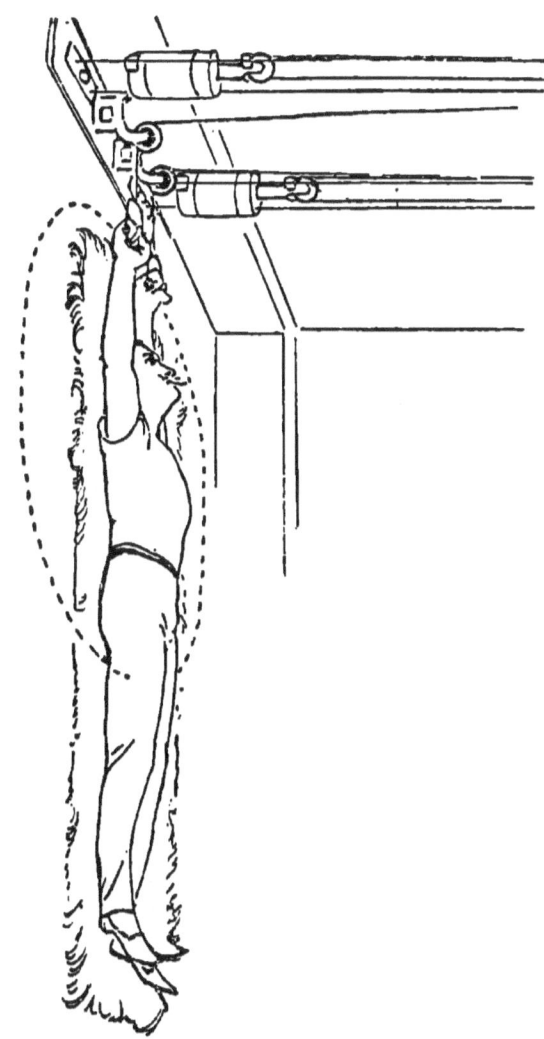

27. Let hands follow dotted lines six or eight counts.
at first, and increase later.

This movement exercises intercostal muscles, and
tends to increase the breadth of chest.

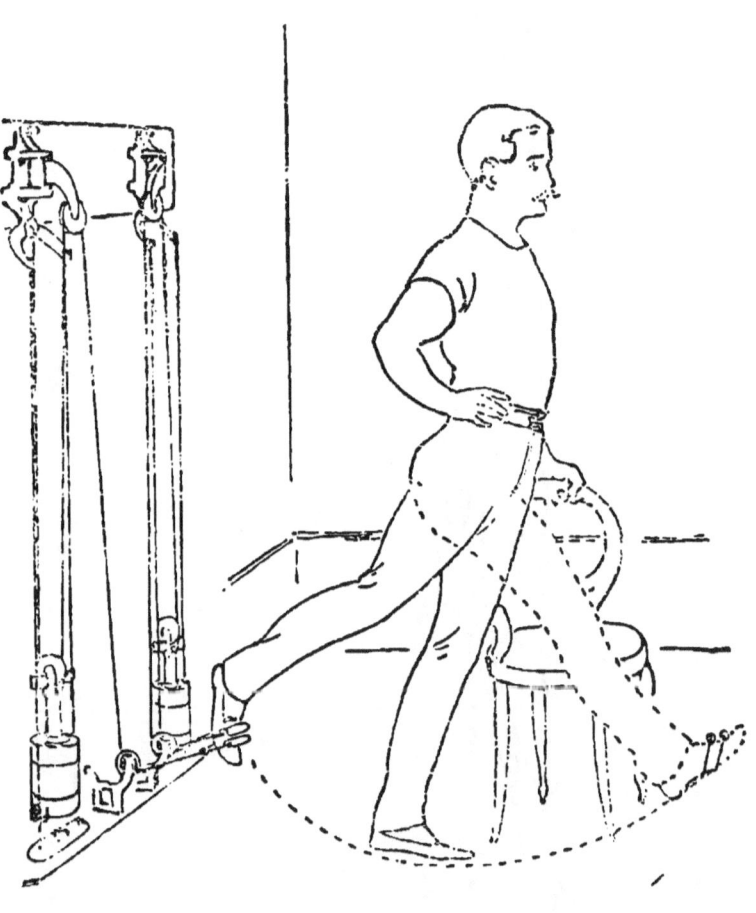

28. Carry leg forward and back slowly. Both legs. Exercises front thigh; sensation similar to that of wading fast through deep water.

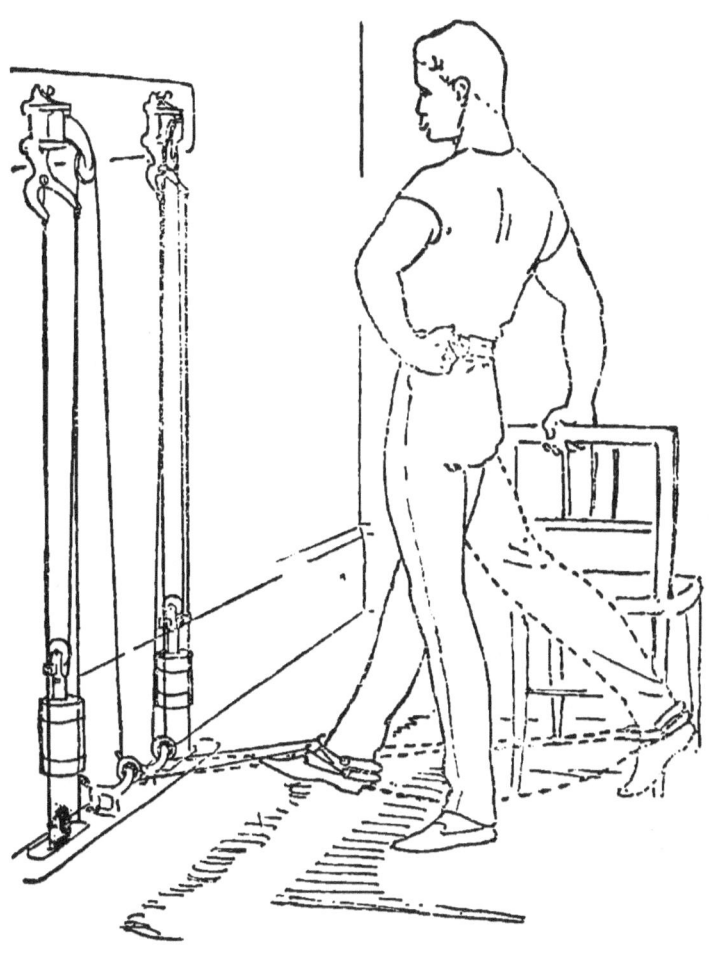

29. Carry leg back and forth slowly. Both legs. Exercises back thigh.

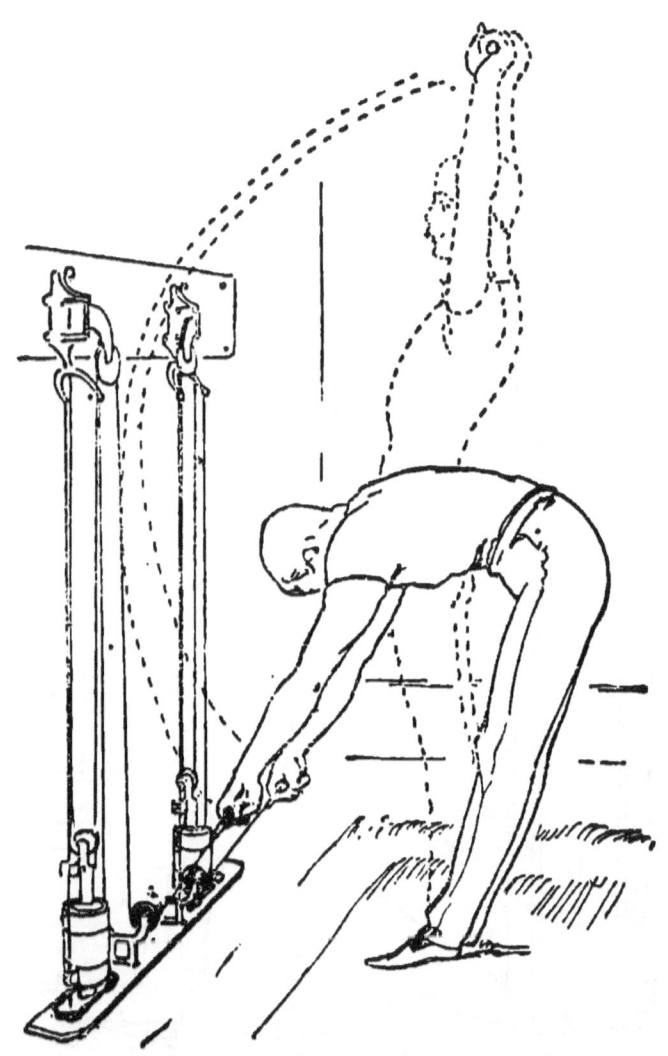

30. Bend body over as far as possible, bending only
in hips. Knees straight. Let arms start up first, and
after they have come in line with torse, biceps touching
ears, keep that relative position, and straighten up to
full height. Six or eight counts at first. To be
recommended for kidney complaint. Exercises small of
back.

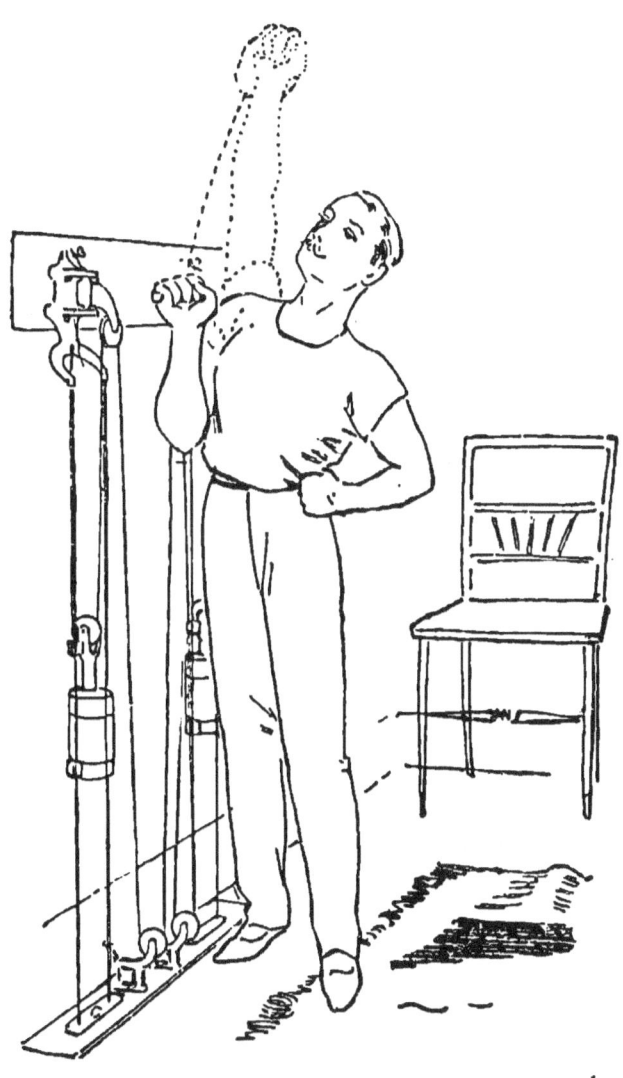

31. Similar to hoisting dumb-bells. Right and left arm should be developed equally. This movement exercises triceps and shoulders.

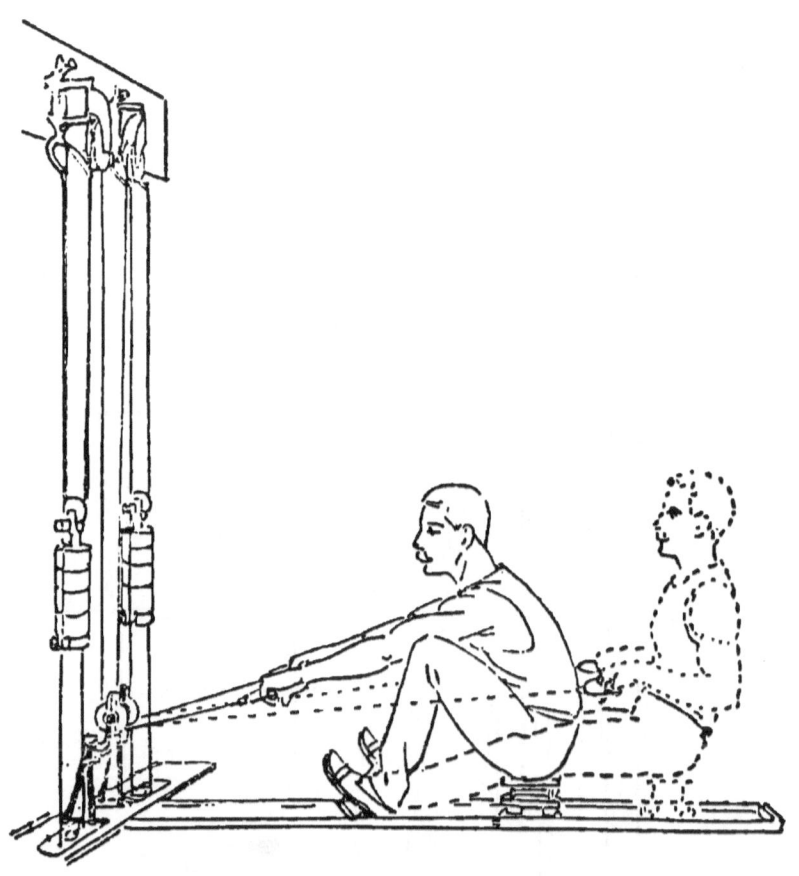

FIFTH SERIES.
(Rowing Attachment.)

32. Keep torse erect; straighten legs first, and then draw arms back, as in cut above. Sixteen counts or more.

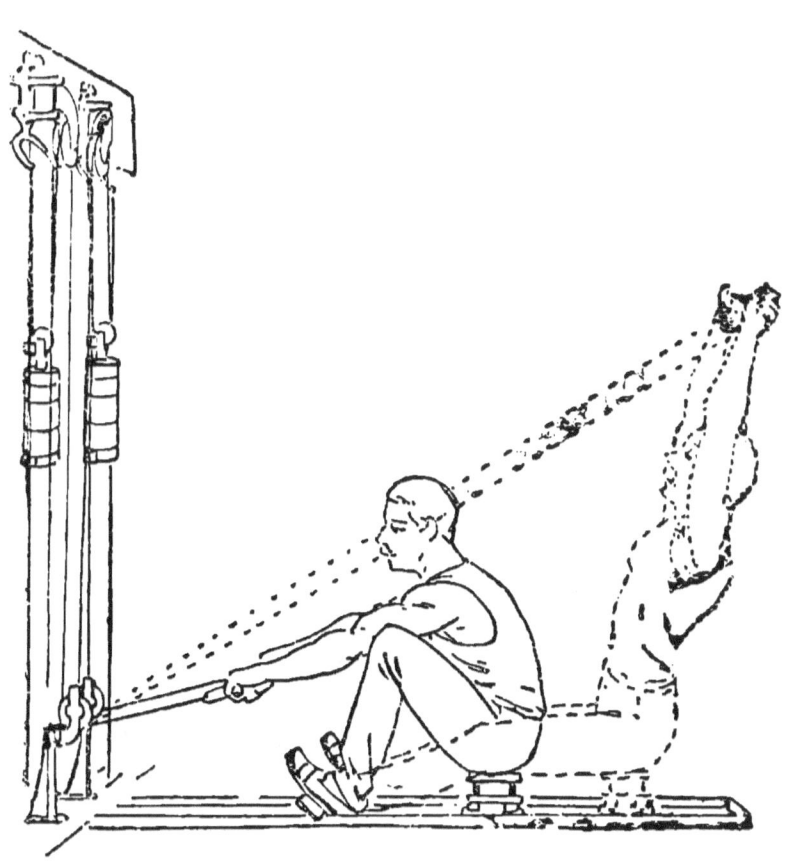

33. Arms, stiff, should move up and backward at same time that the legs are straightening.

As arms go up they should touch the ears, and should not bend throughout the movement.

(a) Take this and previous exercise alternately.

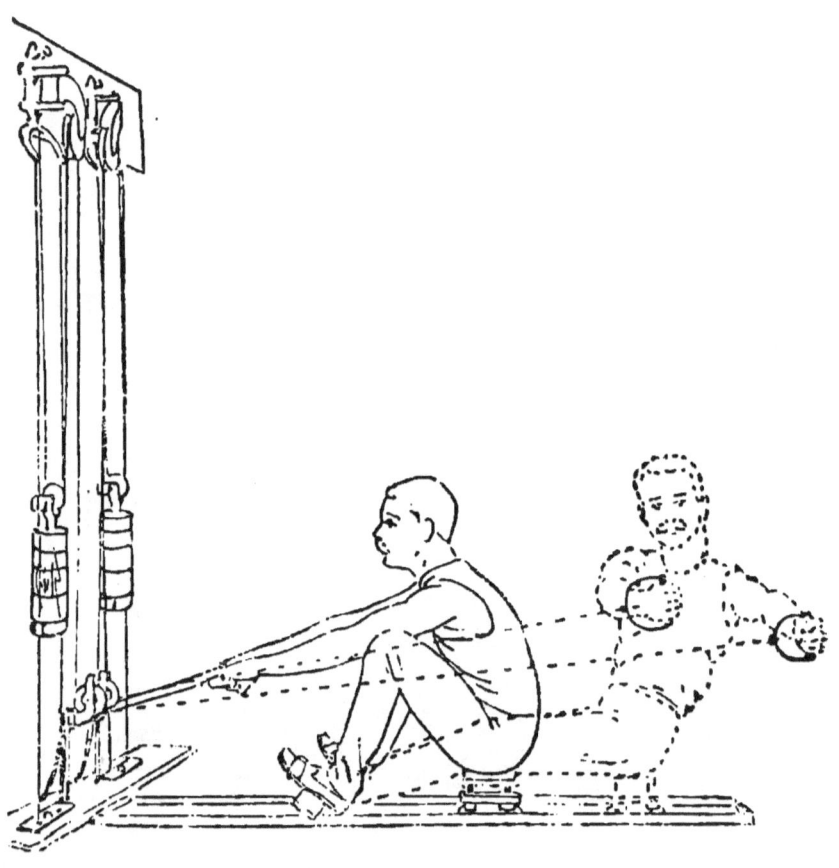

34. Arms swing to side horizontal simultaneously
with straightening of the legs.   Alternate to right and
left side.   Observe same precaution as in No. 7.

35. Stiff arms start to side horizontal simultaneously with the straightening of the legs. Excellent exercise for round shoulders.

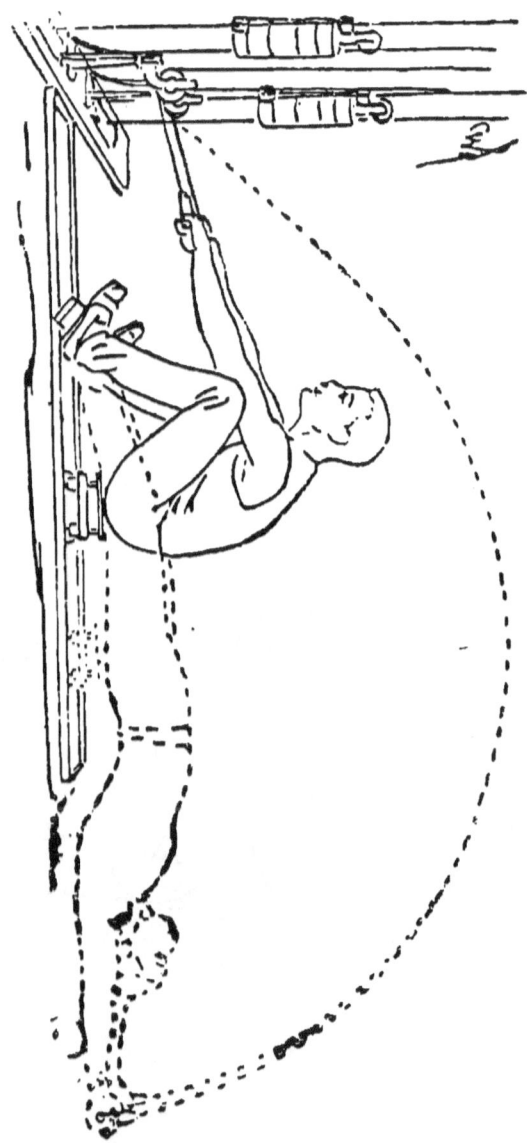

36. Stiff arms start up and backward simultaneously with the straightening of the legs.

(*a*) The abdominal muscles can be more severely

exercised by letting go the weight-handles; fold arms across chest, and let body swing over and back, as in cut.

(b) Or still more severely, by letting go the handles, straightening arms overhead, and letting body take motion as in cut.

(c) Any two of these rowing exercises may be combined alternately, with great advantage.

www.ingramcontent.com/pod-product-compliance
Lightning Source LLC
Chambersburg PA
CBHW022205020726
47496CB00008B/2891